Patty and the Pink Princesses

by Teddy Slater   Illustrated by Sally Springer

SCHOLASTIC INC.
New York Toronto London Auckland Sydney
Mexico City New Delhi Hong Kong Buenos Aires

For Linda Dickey, Bonnie Dry, and Lucie Harris — princesses all.
— T.S.

For Cassidee, my little princess pal.
— S.S.

ISBN-13: 978-0-439-89707-5
ISBN-10: 0-439-89707-6
Text copyright © 2007 by Teddy Slater.
Illustrations copyright © 2007 by Sally Springer.
All rights reserved. Published by Scholastic Inc.
SCHOLASTIC and associated logos are trademarks and/or registered trademarks of Scholastic Inc.

12 11 10 9 8 7 6 5 4 3   7 8 9 10 11 12/0

Printed in the U.S.A.
First printing, January 2007

In the middle of the school year, Patty's family moved.
Suddenly, Patty had a new house, a new school,
and a new teacher.

Everyone in her class had been there since September.
They all knew one another. Patty didn't know anyone.
She missed her old friends.

"Don't worry," Patty's mother said. "I'm sure
you'll make lots of new friends here."
Patty hoped she was right.

Emma, Sophie, Hallie, and Rose were the most popular girls in the class. They always wore something pink to school. At recess, they always played "Princess." They belonged to a special club. It was called the Pink Princesses.

Patty's favorite color was pink.
Her favorite story was
The Princess and the Pea.
She even had her own tiara!
"Can I join your club?" she asked Emma.

Emma looked at Sophie. Sophie looked at Hallie. Hallie looked at Rose. Then they all looked at Patty.

Emma shook her head.

"Sorry," she said. But she didn't sound sorry at all.

"Only real princesses can join."

"How do you know I'm *not* a real princess?" Patty asked.
"Because you don't have blonde hair," Emma said.
The other girls nodded their blonde heads.

"You don't have blue eyes, either," Sophie chimed in.
"Real princesses always have blonde hair and blue eyes."

"But I can't help what color eyes I have," Patty said.
"Well, neither can we," Rose said.

Patty thought that was a mean thing to say.
She couldn't think of anything to say back.

The four girls stared at Patty with their big blue eyes. Then they walked away. They didn't even say good-bye.

Patty wondered why the Pink Princesses didn't
want her in their club. She didn't believe it was
just because of the way she looked.
She thought there must be something else wrong with her.

Patty didn't really like the Pink Princesses anymore.
But she still felt bad that they didn't like her.

How would you feel if you were left out of a group?